PLANET OMAR

ACCIDENTAL TROUBLE MAGNET

BIG-HEARTED, FUNNY AND VERY ENTERTAINING

THE BOOKSELLER

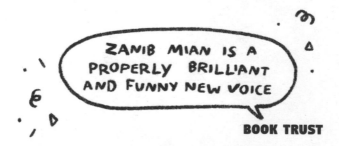

ZANIB MIAN IS A PROPERLY BRILLIANT AND FUNNY NEW VOICE

BOOK TRUST

ZANIB MIAN

ILLUSTRATED BY
NASAYA MAFARIDIK

PLANET OMAR

ACCIDENTAL TROUBLE MAGNET

Hodder

This book was previously published under the title THE MUSLIMS
– the text has since been revised and re-illustrated.
This edition first published in Great Britain in 2019 by Hodder and Stoughton

10

Text copyright © Zanib Mian, 2019
Illustrations copyright © Nasaya Mafaridik, 2019

The moral rights of the author and illustrator have been asserted.

A CIP catalogue record for this book
is available from the British Library.

ISBN 978 1 44495 122 6

Printed and bound in Great Britain
by Clays Ltd, Elcograf S.p.A.
The paper and board used in this book
are made from wood from responsible sources.

MIX
Paper from
responsible sources
FSC® C104740

Hodder Children's Books
An imprint of
Hachette Children's Group
Part of Hodder and Stoughton
Carmelite House
50 Victoria Embankment
London EC4Y 0DZ

An Hachette UK Company
www.hachette.co.uk

www.hachettechildrens.co.uk

This book is dedicated to all

the children who ever felt that

being different is a negative thing.

MARYAM

Thirteen
(but thinks she's sixteen)

13

× 16

Knows 28 surahs
of the Qur'an
by heart

القرآن

Was once caught hiding
a stash of fondant
fancies under her pillow

Loves to wind me up even more
than she loves fondant fancies

MUM

Doesn't know how to say 'no'

A scientist

Hardly ever seen without a cup of coffee in her hands!

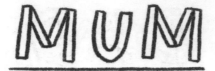

This is what she looks like without her hijab on, when there are no men around who would be allowed to marry her if she didn't already have my dad

DAD

Has a beard because he's copying the greatest man who ever lived — I've never actually seen his face without it

Will never eat a beetroot

Also a scientist

Not too much hair left (he says it's because of his genes)

Rides a motorbike (Grandma tries to puncture the wheels because she doesn't think it's safe)

KHAA

CHAPTER 1

TOOoo!

There was a big puddle
of spit on my little
brother's forehead.

It was mine.

But, **PHEW**, he was still sleeping.

Let me tell you what happened: I had been in my bed, attempting to have a good night's sleep, when suddenly I was being chased through the playground by a teacher who had 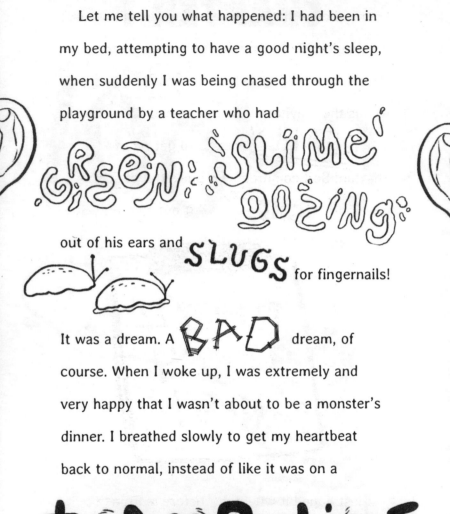 GREEN SLIME OOZING out of his ears and SLUGS for fingernails!

It was a dream. A BAD dream, of course. When I woke up, I was extremely and very happy that I wasn't about to be a monster's dinner. I breathed slowly to get my heartbeat back to normal, instead of like it was on a

 tRAMPoLiNE.

I remembered that my mum told me to spit towards my shoulder three times if I have a nightmare. That's supposed to get rid of SHAYTAN, who is the uglyhead who causes bad dreams. I REALLY wanted to get rid of Shaytan! So I conjured up a bucketful of spit in my mouth SHOT and it out over my left shoulder.

THAT'LL TEACH HIM!

I just hoped it would dry before morning so nobody would know I'd spat on my little brother by accident.

I put my head back on the pillow for an eighth of a second, but then I heard a really loud and really annoying sound.

(See? VERY loud and VERY annoying.)

It was Esa. I guess he'd noticed the spit ball after all and wasn't impressed.

Mum appeared at the door to our room in her pyjamas, looking all bleary-eyed.

(UNIMPRESSED PARENT
CAN BE RECOGNISED BY
HAND ON HIP AND
FURROWED EYEBROWS.
CAN BE SCARY, BUT DO
NOT RUN AWAY.)

She said, 'What's the matter, Esa?'

Esa was still busy wailing, so I said, 'Spit ball.'

'Not again, Omar!'

WAAAAAAAAAA

I covered my head with the pillow.

Then Dad came in saying that it would be nice

if we could have **AT LEAST 1** *night* in the week where poor

Esa isn't woken up by my

SHENANIGANS.

I asked him what that means for the BILLIONTH time. He rolled his eyes for the BILLIONTH time.

I heard my big sister, Maryam, growling in her room. (She definitely doesn't like mornings very much.)

Mum said it was almost Fajr time anyway. I wondered if Allah was going to give me a reward for waking them up for Fajr.

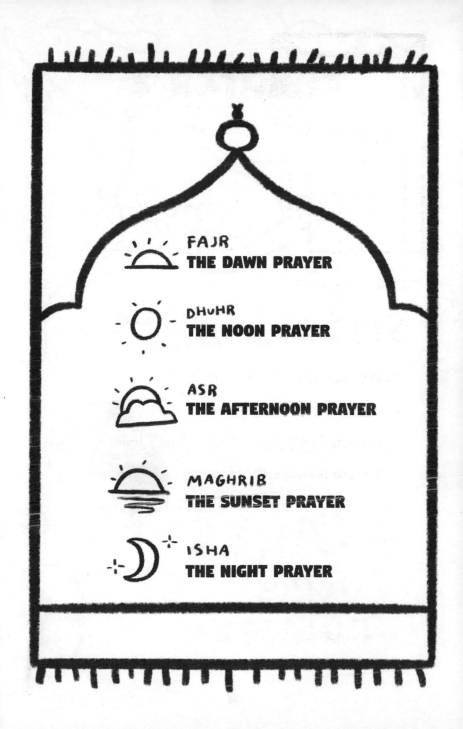

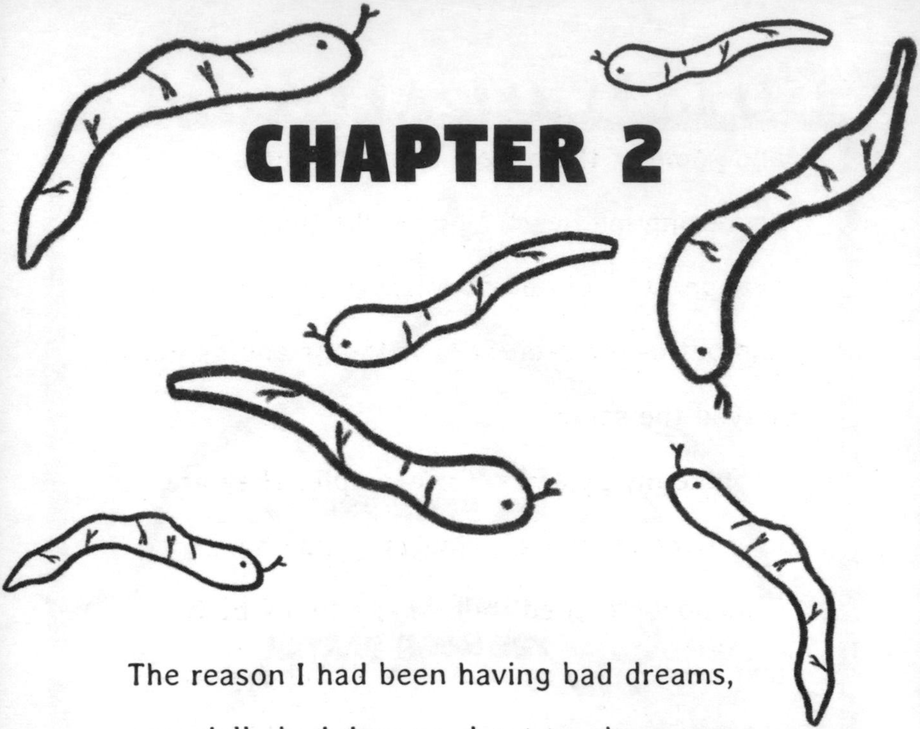

CHAPTER 2

The reason I had been having bad dreams,

especially bad dreams about teachers, was

because I was going to be

starting a new school. This

made me feel like there were

SNAKES
in my
TUMMY

and some of them were sneaking up and squeezing my heart. I don't like things to change. It would be so much more convenient and better for everybody if things always just stayed the same.

Take my pyjamas, for example. They are utterly comfortable pyjamas, which have somehow moulded their shape to my body and become my second skin. A weird second skin that I can take off and put on, like some

kind of cool human lizard. My mum tried to throw them away and make me wear crispy pyjamas that

DON'T EVEN HAVE DINOSAURS ON THEM

This is change. It's super annoying.

One big, fat, huge change had already

happened to me. We had to move house, which

is the reason I had to start at a new school. All

this happened because Mum got her

When she told me, I couldn't help wondering

what she meant exactly by

Did it mean that adults have super boring

dreams all about jobs? If that was true, I

wasn't looking forward to being an adult,

because at the moment I dream about fun stuff,

like being on a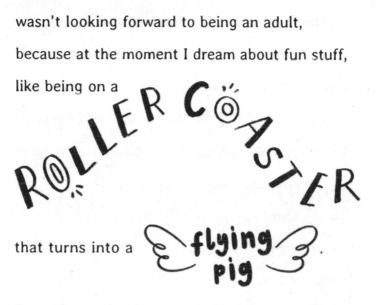

that turns into a flying pig.

Sometimes, they're even better than movies!

Well, apart from the scary ones that make me

feel really lucky when I wake up and realise

they're not for real.

So, anyway, the job that Mum must have

dreamt about all the time was too far from

where we lived before, so we had to move.

The moving bit was very, very X 100

ANNOYING

because Dad said I couldn't put all the 1,267 bits and bobs and toys from my room in the boxes to take to the new house. He didn't actually count my things, but he likes to say exact numbers when he is talking, so he can sound smart. He said I had to choose the ones I love most and give the rest to charity. Why didn't he understand that

I LOVE THEM ALL.

But then he said he would be very proud of me if I could choose, because I would have done better than Mum, who had already packed lots of what Dad called 'boxes of hoarded goods'. I like Dad being proud of me (especially because it normally means *pain au chocolat* for breakfast), so I chose 56 bits and bobs to take with me. I counted them really carefully, so I could be precise when Dad asked (and also make sure that nobody sneakily threw anything away without me noticing).

The good news was that the new house was super, super cool. When we first saw it, Maryam and I ran straight into the garden and whooped, because it was at least twice the size of our old one. We planned out where we could put a football net and Esa's climbing frame and Maryam did loads of cartwheels to prove just how massive it was.

WOOO HOOO YAY!

That was the first time we saw the little old lady who lives next door. She peeped over her fence and said, 'Humph.' And she put her nose higher in the air as if she was smelling something there that she didn't like.

HUMPH!

CHAPTER 3

School was going to start on Monday. Only
two more sleeps before I had to walk into a
brand-new classroom with everyone watching
and a teacher who might or might not be an

ALIEN
ZOMBIE

Saturday is always mosque day. My mum had decided that for the first few weeks after moving we would visit a different mosque every Saturday and pray Dhuhr there, to see what our new neighbourhood was like. Dad normally works on Saturdays, so it was just me, Maryam, Esa and Mum.

My mum is a **VERY SMART SCIENTIST**

and works out all sorts of different ways of fighting cancer for the cancer research people. But sometimes Esa's cuteness makes her lose her smartness.

IT'S LIKE HE HAS *big, innocent, smartness-melting eyes*

They don't work on me, so when Esa wanted
to buy a whistle from the petrol station on
the way to the mosque, I knew it wasn't a
good idea. But Mum went right ahead and
bought it for him, saying, 'Because you've
been such a good boy this morning!' and
giving him a

GOOEY
KISS

on the top of his head. I knew it was gooey
because she actually still kisses me like that,
even though I've forbidden her to do it in
front of my friends.

In the mosque, everyone prays together with the imam leading. It's supposed to be *super quiet*. Just after the prayer began, Esa decided to move from his place. I was praying in between Mum and Maryam. Neither of them moved. I wasn't sure if they'd even noticed that he'd got up.

Now, Esa is annoying sometimes, but he IS my little brother, and I worry about him, so I quickly sneaked a look behind us. He was sitting at the back with

A BIG CHEEKY GRIN

on his face. I turned back around and carried on praying. Then we went into Rukhu. That's when your hands are on your knees. Silence from Esa. Then we went into Sujood. That's when your nose and forehead are on the ground.

RUKHU

SUJOOD

And then ...

TWEEEEE!

The loud noise of a whistle broke through the silence, followed by Esa's voice: 'One, two, three, four, five!' Then again:

And then the counting. It wouldn't stop.

I couldn't help myself. How could I? I

BURST OUT LAUGHING!

right in the middle of my prayer. I put my hand over my mouth. I bit my tongue and

I even pinched myself really hard, but I couldn't help it! I didn't have to wonder if Mum had heard. People on all floors of the mosque must have heard.

When the prayer finished, Mum and Maryam were a bright shade of pink. It looked as if their skin had suddenly decided to

compete with Maryam's socks for pinkness.

And they were looking everywhere except up at people's faces like they usually do when they greet people after prayers. Mum was

motioning angrily to Esa to come to her.
Luckily, a few people came and patted Esa's
head, which made Mum's skin return to its
normal colour.

As we were leaving, an old lady with a
walking stick and brown abaya waddled over
and said:

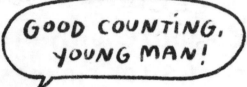

GOOD COUNTING, YOUNG MAN!

CHAPTER 4

Sunday passed pretty quickly, because

Sundays are science days. Dad calls them

SCIENCE SUNDAYS

in one of those big BOOMING

voices, like it's the most fun you could ever

have on a Sunday. Why? Because my dad is

also a scientist, and I think he and my mum

only had us three kids so that they could

create more scientists or something.

I actually like science so I don't mind.

We always do fun things, like making slime,

creating fizzy eruptions and making things go

There are four things that pretty much seem to happen on every Science Sunday:

1. Mum wants everything done **VERy** precisely, she's obsessive about it, but pretends that she's not, because Science Sundays are supposed to be fun, and not bossy. She ends up saying things like, 'Just 1ml more, my cotton button,' through gritted teeth. And, 'Are you sure you stirred that correctly, sunshine?'

2. Dad laughs at just how crazy Mum gets about the preciseness. And he kisses her head and says that's why she's the best scientist in the world. And she kisses his hand and smiles like she's the luckiest woman in the world

(SUPER YUCK!).

3. Maryam **ALWAYS** drops important parts of the experiment on the floor.

4. Esa **ALWAYS** steps on the important parts of the experiment that Maryam drops on the floor. This is because he has **ants in his pants**

and in his shoes and **EVERYWHERE,** and he can't stay still, **EVER.**

That Sunday, we did

tornados in bottles, which is

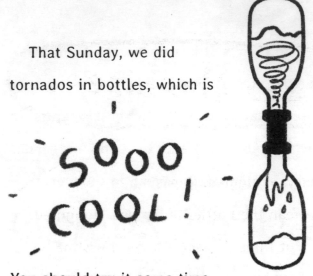

SOOO
COOL!

You should try it some time.

You connect two bottles with a little pipe

and you whirl the top bottle, which makes

the water go down to the bottom bottle, and

sends air up, making a tornado.

We all set the things up together, on the

kitchen table.

My brain was thinking about telling

Maryam to pass the bottles and pipes, but my

mouth hadn't caught up with my brain yet

and got things muddled up, so it came out as,

Pass the bipes!

Maryam giggled. 'Bipes?'

'I mean the bottles and pipes.' I giggled, too. 'But I like it. BIPES. I wish it was a real word.'

'If it was a real word, then it would just be normal and you wouldn't like it any more,' said Maryam.

'That's so true,' I said.

Mum and Dad were bending over laughing in the corner of the kitchen. When we asked them what was so funny, they said that in the Arabic language, there's no 'p' sound, so a pipe would end up being called a 'bibe'.

Then Maryam, who was showing off

Googling with her smartphone, said that

actually Bipes are a type of

WEIRD DISGUSTING SNAKE-LIZARD

type thing, that look like they're inside out.

Eventually, we got on with the experiment.

'Oh yeah, tornado in a bottle!' said Dad.

Sometimes he gets really cheesy and excited,

and Maryam and I look at each other and roll

our eyes. (But we kind of like it, really.)

'You can put glitter or food colouring in

the bottle too, to see the tornado better,'

said Mum, so Maryam and Esa both reached

for the glitter, and Maryam dropped the

bottle on the floor, sending glitter flying

E-V-E-R-Y-W-H-E-R-E.

'Right on schedule,' said Dad with a peal of laughter. Mum hugged Maryam and kissed her, also giggling uncontrollably. I could see that Maryam wasn't taking it well.

'URGH!'

She shrugged Mum off and stomped towards the stairs. 'Science is so lame anyway.'

She does extra grumpy things like that a lot at the moment. Although it's not like she's ALWAYS grumpy, sometimes she's the nice Maryam too. It's weird. Dad says it's teenage hormones.

CHAPTER 5

When I woke up on Monday morning, I felt like my lungs were pushing air out of me and not taking any back in, and my stomach was a

GIANT HEAVY ROCK

making it impossible for me to get out of bed.

REASONS I WAS NERVOUS

what if nobody
likes me?

$$\{ 1/X \, [-10,10,-5,5] \}$$

what if the work
is harder than
at my last school?

what if nobody
wants to be my
friend?

what if the teacher
is an alien?

Maryam poked her head around the door and said, 'Hurry up, *lazyhead* and stop pretending to be sick.'

I wasn't.

I wondered how her lungs felt. She was acting pretty Maryam-like, so her lungs seemed to be normal.

Then Dad appeared at the door too, and gave her one of his cheeky looks, which made his face look like he knew a secret. He came in and tickled me and threw me over his right shoulder, like he was kidnapping me, then carried me downstairs and plunked me down in front of a bowl of porridge. Now, I know what you might be thinking ... YUCK!

But actually, when you put biscuit spread

into your bowl of porridge, it tastes very

(Though I'm only allowed one spoonful of the

biscuit spread.)

I ate slowly, because of the rock in my

tummy. Mum said it would be OK and the

teacher would make sure I made friends.

I DRAGGED MY LEADS UP↑ THE STAIRS

(USED TO BE KNOWN AS LEGS UNTIL THEY GOT SO HEAVY)

I got washed. There was no uniform at this school, so I was allowed to wear what I wanted.

I looked for my **FAVOURITE SWEATSHIRT** and finally pulled it out from the space between my bed and my bedside table. Then I looked for my **FAVOURITE JEANS**

They were exactly where I had left them
– on the floor next to the bookshelf. They
had a stain on them from when Esa threw a
barbeque chicken wing at me. *Oh, well.*
I put them on anyway.

When I went downstairs, my mum went

BARMY

I mean, she took one look at me and
flew off the handle. She said she couldn't
believe it. That's all she said actually.
She said it five times.

Dad said calmly, 'Son, I think Allah has given you clean clothes to wear. So, go and put them on, please, or we'll be late.'

Then he **KIDNAPPED** me on his shoulder again and helped me take out some clothes from my cupboard. I put them on **AS FAST AS HUMANLY POSSIBLE** and ran down the stairs. I flew out of the front door towards the car, where Mum was waiting with a cross look on her face.

CHAPTER 6

The thought of
getting into the car
made my tummy feel
like there were

A MILLION
FROGS

hopping about in it, just waiting to leap up my

throat. So, I took a deep breath and imagined

a better way to get to school ...

ON A
SUPER
Awesome,
Magnificent
DRAGON

I could see him there now, just hovering beside our car and looking at me with a smile. He made me feel better. About everything. The dragon bowed his head and flung open the car door for me, which made me laugh out loud.

'What's so funny, Omar?' Mum asked, one hand still on the handle of the car door.

But I just shook my head and buttoned my lips. My mum NEVER really understands about how to imagine things properly, so there was no point explaining – I guess it's the kind of thing grown-ups forget how to do.

So, I just stared at the dragon's blue and green shimmery scales and long swooping tail. As I strapped myself in, I wondered what it would be like to ride him to school, instead of driving.

HE'D FLY AT LEAST 120MPH

He looked at me with his almond-shaped eyes and let out a puff of steam from his tiny nostrils.

I imagined him riding alongside us all the way to school. When we got out and walked to the gate, I made him breathe out a huge

plume of steam and in my head I said,

'I PRONOUNCE THEE H_2O!'

as if I were a  or something.

I thought that was a good name for him

because steam is made from water and H_2O is

the chemical name for water (that's the kind

of science-y thing my parents L♡VE

to talk about).

So, there I was. The new kid in

the class. I was petrified and my

lungs were still doing that

funny thing. I made them

feel better by imagining

H_2O being silly

at the window. He

STUCK HIS TONGUE OUT

Then he put bits of **POPCORN**

in each of his nostrils and blew them out.

The teacher, who was called Mrs
Hutchinson, introduced me to the class. She
was what my mum would call a pear-shaped
person. I liked her hair from the first time I
saw her, and later learned that the springy
auburn curls reacted to her mood and told
the story of her day. When she was happy,
those curls were happy. They would bounce
merrily out of her head like

When she was tired, they would flop down lazily on her cheeks. And when she was cross, they looked more like the twisty metal part of a drill. Sometimes, when she was angry, I would imagine a drill-headed Mrs Hutchinson making a big hole in the wall quite easily.

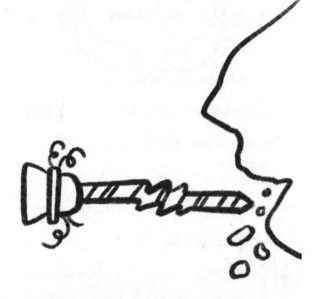

She asked me to sit down next to a red-headed kid called Charlie. Charlie had lots of freckles all over his face, and thick-

rimmed glasses. I thought he looked cool,
so I smiled at him. He smiled back at me. He
was missing one of his front teeth.

Charlie told me the school was OK.
The lessons were OK. The playground
was OK when it wasn't wet. And Mrs
Hutchinson's class was mostly filled with
OK kids. Except for Daniel. (I decided that
'OK' was Charlie's favourite word.)

'Daniel is the one who you have to look
out for, OK? Just stay out of his way.'
'OK,' I said.

I thought about all the times my mum had told me to stay away from something which seemed to make me drawn towards it like a

MAGNET

instead. Like when **I JUST HAD TO** open Maryam's secret box, because I was told I wasn't allowed to, and when I did, a gazillion teeny, tiny beads came pouring out, all over her bedroom floor, just as she walked in.

I GULPED.

CHAPTER 7

I thought I was going to get through the day without any

Until lunchtime, that is.

Daniel bounded up to Charlie and me and said, 'The new kid and the weird kid sitting together. How

"NICE".

He said 'nice' in a different way to when people normally say it. I wondered if it was sarcasm, but my sarcasm detector isn't very good. I can get confused when people say things all

UPSIDE DOWN.

I tried to figure out if actually Daniel wasn't as bad as Charlie had warned and he *did* think it was nice that we were sitting together, or if he was being mean, because it obviously wasn't very nice of him to call Charlie 'the weird kid'.

Anyway, Mum and Dad say to always think about things before blurting them out.

I could feel Charlie trying to think of what to say, too. He was taking air into his lungs really deeply, as if he was preparing to say something, and then opening his mouth and closing it again, but nothing came out.

I think we were both silent for a super-long time, which seemed to make Daniel very cross. He shouted,

¡DIoTS!

before walking away.

When he was gone, Charlie said, 'See?
He's always horrible to me.'

'Why?' I asked. 'Did you two have a fight
about something?'

'No. He just hates me for no reason. I
think he hates the whole class, but he hates
me the most.'

Charlie looked so sad, and so small, I
couldn't help putting my arm around him
which made Charlie look at me and smile his

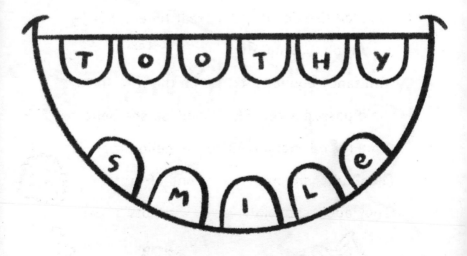

When Mum picked me up later, I told her all about my new friend. I saw her breathe a 'phew'. I guess she was worried about how good or not good my first day would be since I was so nervous. I also told her that I liked Mrs Hutchinson and her

amazing changing hair.

Mum told me about her day, too. It sounded like she'd had a great time at her dream job, poking at MICROSCOPIC STUFF with fancy equipment. And on the way home she'd passed a chocolate shop, so she bought some for our neighbour to say hello properly. Thankfully, she had bought one of those fancy adult chocolate boxes with lots of dark

chocolates in, which are so yuck that I didn't wish the box was for me instead, which I normally do when we have to give chocolate to other people.

'I thought we could pop round when we get home!'

'OK,' I said slowly, remembering how grumpy the neighbour had been last time I saw her.

We picked up Maryam and the

little human thing we call a brother,

who always comes home from nursery with half his lunch on his jumper. Mum had to neaten Esa up before we popped over next door, because she's embarrassed to have mucky kids.

She even said to me, 'Wait. Let me hair your run through my fingers.'

ha ha ha ha ha! ˆ◡ˆ

Mum says things the wrong way round when she's hurrying.

'You mean *run your fingers through his hair*,' said Maryam, because she likes to correct people.

'Yes, yes, that,' said Mum and she marched us all over and took a deep breath and rang the doorbell.

We waited.

NOTHING!

We waited some more.

NOTHING!

So I reached forward and rapped on the door, really loud, a few times.

'Why did you do that?' Mum hissed like a quiet, angry snake.

'What?' I shrugged. 'Maybe the doorbell isn't working?'

'Well, it's rude,' hissed snake-Mum, and just then the door opened quietly and eerily, like in horror movies.

There stood an old lady. Quite a short one. With lots of white hair and one of those cardigans that all old ladies wear. My grandma has one.

We all said 'Hi' pretty much together,
except Esa, who said,

`Assalamu 'alaikum'`

like he had been taught to say to our nani.
The old lady was really weird, because
she just stood there without
reacting. She didn't say
hello. She just stared.

Mum explained that we
were the new neighbours.

The old lady stared.

Mum said, 'We just
thought we'd come
over to introduce
ourselves.'

The old lady stared.

Maryam gave me a secret whack on the

arm, which was meant to say:

OMG, THIS IS SO AWKWARD!

I gave her a secret whack back, which was

meant to say:

OMG, I KNOW!

Then Mum asked the creepy, rude next-

door-neighbour what her name was.

Just when we thought she wouldn't say

anything, she blurted out, 'Rogers,' then slammed the door.

I glanced up at Mum. She looked like one of those helium balloons that hardly has any helium left in it at all.

CHAPTER 8

For a few mornings, as we left for school,

my mum asked me if I had done my duas. My

mum is absolutely

OBSESSED

with having a

routine that we stick

to every morning

– a bit like it's

one of her science

experiments.

    My parents do their duas whenever they

think of something they want to talk to Allah

about. I sometimes wonder if other people

see a Muslim's lips moving and think they're

✦ SECRETLY CASTING ✦ A SPELL ✦

or just talking to themselves, when actually

they're just doing one of their duas.

There are duas for everything:

eating **SLeePiNG**

WAKiNG uP

PROTECTiÖN

knowledge

leaving the house 🏠🤲

coming back into the house 🏠🤲

Basically, anything you can think of.

I used to forget them sometimes, but now I was making sure I did them as soon as I woke up. Especially the prayer for

⁞ PROTECTION ⁞

because Daniel was getting meaner every day and I felt like I needed all the help I could get.

He had started to follow Charlie and me around the playground at break times. Sometimes he wouldn't say anything, but he would do lots of staring and make grunting noises, as if he was having some really mean thoughts. And once,

HE CHARGED

Then started laughing like mad because
it made Charlie jump.

Minus Daniel, school was getting to be
quite all right, especially since Charlie and
me were becoming super best friends. We
laughed at all the same things, and we even
wished for all the same things, like getting
an Xbox and more screen time to go with it.
That was starting to make up for how much
I missed my friends back at my old school.
I was still a bit worried that they might be
forgetting about me, but Dad said we could
all get together in the holidays.

AT US LIKE A RHINO

Mrs Hutchinson was really nice, too. Every time she saw me in the mornings, or when she walked past my desk, she checked on me and gave me a **WINK!**

$$\widehat{●} \underset{\smile}{} \widehat{<}$$

Not all the lessons were fun, obviously, but whenever we did something creative she got really enthusiastic and her curls were happy and bouncy. It made me wonder if maybe she could imagine things the way I did, or if she was just like all the other adults.

One afternoon, when we were doing an art lesson about Picasso, Mrs Hutchinson was so excited about how he made everything abstract that her curls started dancing with joy. She asked us to paint self-portraits just like his. Charlie and I were having loads of fun giving ourselves colourful triangle noses and weird-shaped eyes, when Daniel walked past our desk and sent the dirty water pot tumbling onto my painting.

'Oops, clumsy me ...'

There he was again with the upside-down talking. It definitely wasn't an *oops* moment, it was a

Charlie's mouth dropped open in surprise and my heart took a little dip, as if it was

falling into a different and less comfy place in my chest.

It seemed like Charlie could tell exactly how I was feeling. Because he leaned in to whisper, 'He's just a big

FROGSPAWN

head. I bet you can paint a new one even better!' And he gave me the biggest toothy grin I'd seen yet.

I imagined what Picasso looked like. I wondered if he looked like some of his paintings, all out of shape, but happy. Happier than all the other paintings from those old days. And then I thought,

HEY, WHAT IF SOME KID HAD RUINED PICASSO'S PAINTING AT SCHOOL ONE DAY, WHICH IS WHY IT CAME OUT ALL DIFFERENT AND WEIRD AND THAT'S WHAT MADE HIM FAMOUS?

So I took my paintbrush, I grabbed it like it was alive and like it was the first time I ever held a paintbrush, and I painted.

When Mrs Hutchinson saw my work, her curls almost rose to the ceiling.

'Omar, Omar,' she said.

'Yes, Miss.'

'It's ... wow. It's brilliant!'

Daniel's face was red. Like the beetroots my dad will never eat. He passed me a note.

It said:

When Mum came to pick me up, he stared at us both as if we were someone's old

chewing gum,

that he had accidently touched under the desk. I almost pointed him out to her, but then I remembered how relieved she'd been that I thought school was OK, and I kept quiet.

Sometimes, though, I think my mum magically knows when somebody in her family needs cheering up, because that evening she announced she was making biryani.

Biryani is my all-time favourite Pakistani food.

It's hard to make and Mum says scientists with full-time jobs don't have the time to make it every week, like I had asked her to.

Mum always opens the French doors to the patio when she is cooking, no matter how cold it is outside, because she can't stand the house to smell of food. Homes are meant to smell of nothing, she says,

NOT FISH,

NOT SAMOSAS,

NOT SMELLY SOCKS

and not even weird, artificial air fresheners.
And since the door was open, I stood there
with my giant bubble kit to see if I could
really make a bubble bigger than me, like it
said on the packet.

I could see our next-door-neighbour, the
horrible Mrs Rogers. She was outside, poking
around at her weeds with one wrinkly hand
and holding her phone with the other.

After a few minutes, we heard her say
loudly:

'Oh, I'm with her on this one,' joked Dad, who hates it when the smell of frying onion and garlic gets into his clothes.

'I know, I knowwwww. We don't want to give her another reason not to like us!' said Mum. Then she held Dad's arm, like she does when she is going to tell him a really good idea.

'Let's send her some! She'll love it! ♡'

I know it gets really stinky when the biryani is cooking, but SERIOUSLY, it's so yummy. It's worth it!

I couldn't believe that Mum was being so nice

after the way Mrs Rogers treated us when
we took her those chocolates. Why did she
deserve some of our delicious dinner?

And to make it worse, Mum and Dad made
Maryam and me take it round to her house.
She took ages to open the door, as usual. And
when she finally did and we tried to give her
the container, she just said, 'Spicy food???
No thank you!' as she closed the door.

'Sheeeeeeesh,' said Maryam.
'You'd think we
were trying to
poison her.'

CHAPTER 9

Mum and Dad were so happy that I was getting on well at school that they said I could invite Charlie over. They obviously didn't know the bit about me not actually getting on well at school **100%** because Daniel made most days **40%** bad. Well, depending on how much he felt like a big, huge grump that day, he sometimes made them **60%** bad.

I wondered why he was worse on some days and I imagined him walking to school and slipping on **ROTTEN APPLES.**

If you've ever seen a rotten apple, you'll
know that they're really sludgy and soft and
can make you fall right down if you ever step
on one, even more than a banana skin. So,
the more rotten apples he slipped on, the
worse he felt, and the more mean he was.
That could be it. **THERE HAD TO
BE SOMETHING.**

Charlie was mega excited about coming
over. I asked him if he wanted to have pizza
and he said yes, which is what I knew he
would say, because every kid loves pizza.
(Unless they're allergic to cheese, like my
cousin Faiza, who does lots of farts and gets
really bad tummy aches if she eats it.)

Charlie told me all about the flavours that
he hates tasting in food, but luckily none of
them are on pizzas:

- Peanut
- Coconut
- Banana
- Cinnamon
- Coffee

Charlie was very polite to my mum and
dad when he came over. He said extra pleases
and thank yous. And he smiled an extra lot.

'I've been hearing so much about you,
Charlie,' said Mum.

'Oh, thank you,' said Charlie.

'It's so nice to have you over, and you can come any time you want,' said Dad.

I imagined them as blocks of cheese, the holey kind that they draw in cartoons but which I've never actually tasted.

Maryam decided to hang about near us and show off like she always does. The weird thing about it was that Charlie actually *liked* her.

She even came with us to play football in the garden. She used to play football normally, but recently she's started giggling a lot and celebrating with loud

YAYS

It's super annoying. Charlie didn't seem to mind though. He laughed right along with her, the way he does with me, but not really with many other people in the class.

All this laughing made Mrs Rogers come into her garden to investigate. She must have been on the phone, because she was talking to the person called John again.

'I CAN HEAR THE MUSLIMS. THEY'RE BEING NOISY AGAIN, JOHN.'

JOHN
03:54

She said it very loudly.

'I mean really, why can't they play quietly like good children? I can't take this much ridiculous noise.'

We all looked at each other, suddenly silent. We couldn't see her properly over the fence, just the top of her white hair. And then we burst out laughing and ran inside to eat our pizza.

CHAPTER 10

At school, it was getting harder and harder to avoid **Daniel Green.**

One lunchtime, he came over and put a handful of sand all over my food. My stomach clenched and I got a lump in my throat. I didn't want to cry in front of him, but I was really hungry, and that sandwich, from last night's leftover chicken, was really tasty and my mouth had really been looking forward to it.

I quickly imagined H_2O swooping down from the clouds to hover right behind Daniel. I made H_2O pull a totally unimpressed face and blow steam all over Daniel's head. And Daniel had no clue.

That made me laugh and through my giggles I said loudly, 'Thanks, Daniel. Now I truly have a sand-wich.'

A few people around us started laughing too. Sarah and Ellie – girls from our class – were sitting at the lunch table next to ours and they were giggling like crazy.

Daniel stood there towering over me with his podgy fists closed tight. His face was redder than his T-shirt and he was

CLENCHING HIS TEETH

together tightly. I pictured him as a Rottweiler dog, baring his sharp teeth ready for a fight.

At this point I realised that being smart with a bully wasn't very smart at all. Charlie must have realised this too, because he had been sensible enough not to laugh and now he looked like a frightened little lamb.

I quickly muttered the **PROTECTION** dua under my breath.

Then there was a loud growling sound and Daniel was launching his head towards my stomach. I don't know how, but I managed to throw myself onto the floor out of his way. It was all very fast. Daniel's head went into my empty chair, with his huge body following. The force sent the chair flying into the girls

behind us, followed by a 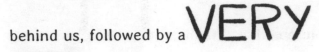VERY

BIG,

VERY

ANGRY

body that ended up on top of Sarah.

I probably don't need to tell you that

Daniel was in BIG FAT

TROUBLE.

He spent one hour in Mr Barnes' class as

punishment. Mr Barnes has a moustache.

A big one. It
looks like it
could come
alive on his
face like a

SLITHERING
SLUG.

By home time, Daniel was back. He still
looked angry. As we queued up to leave the
classroom, he stood behind me and breathed
down my neck.

'Don't think I don't know the worst thing
about you. YOU'RE MUSLIM.
I saw your mum the other day, looking like
a witch, in black. You better go back to your
country before we kick you all out.'

I didn't say a word. I just gulped.

How could anyone think my mum looked like a witch? If I'd been braver, I'd have told Daniel he was stupid not to be able to tell the difference.

eat kids for dinner	would never harm a kid
poisonous wart	wart, if present, is not poisonous
has no hair under wig	has lots of hair under scarf
scowl	♥ smile ♥
ugly, due to horrid thoughts	beautiful, due to lovely thoughts

On the way home,
I couldn't stop thinking
about what Daniel had said.

BEFORE THEY KICK US ALL OUT? WHAAAAT?

I thought about talking to Maryam about

him. Maybe she could help and tell me what

to do, without having to tell our parents. I

know they'd get all stressy and worried and

make a big fuss at school and that would

definitely just make Daniel worse. Maryam

might be annoying, but she used to stand up

for me back when I was a really little kid and we still went to the same school ...

But then I remembered the time just before we moved that I was quietly trying to get away with going over my screen time limit in my room and Dad came stomping in, like a giant who had just stepped on an enormous drawing pin.

I COULD PRACTICALLY SEE THE STEAM COMING OUT OF HIS EARS.

He had discovered the TV remote was missing its batteries. I froze. I didn't move and didn't say a word. I imagined I was a spider playing dead when someone is trying to smack it with a slipper.

Then Maryam came in with her huge, pointy finger of accusation.

HE DID IT!

It was true. I had desperately needed them for my controller ... I got into so much trouble that day. I was banned from video games for a month.

Maryam is a complete snitch these days. No, I couldn't trust her.

CHAPTER 11

I knew there was one person I *could* trust to
talk to about Daniel: my cousin Reza. And,
luckily, we were going up to Manchester to
visit a couple of days after the sand disaster.
I was bursting to ask him whether he'd heard
about Muslims getting kicked out of the
country. Did Daniel just make that part up?
Could it possibly be real?

REZA is SUPER COOL.

He's twelve. He's the kind of kid that
knows a lot about everything. If anything

happens to his bike, he can fix it using his dad's tools, and I've even seen him topping up the oil in his mum's little red car, which he calls a banger. And when we walk around in Manchester with him and his family, lots of people always say, 'Hi.' Reza must have really great pester power skills, or maybe he knows hypnosis, because he literally has everything he wants. That's one of the reasons I love going there because we have two days of playing on his Xbox as much as we want and we always have a *midnight feast* YUM!

I'm pretty sure almost every Muslim has cousins in Manchester. I was wondering if they were all as interesting as mine while I finished packing my rucksack, when my dad shouted up the stairs, 'Get in the Peanut, everyone! We're leaving in two minutes!'

You might be wondering how we could all get into a peanut. We can't. This is what we call the **PEANUT.** It's a 4x4. But look at the number plate!

There are some things that always happen on our road trip to Manchester:

- Mum packs too much food for the journey
- Dad complains when he is putting the luggage in the car
- We always stop at the services and eat hot food, so mum's journey food is uneaten
- Dad says,

"I TOLD YOU SO."

As we were loading the car with all our stuff, Mrs Rogers came out into her front garden to put a bag in the dustbin.

But instead of just going back inside, she

stood and watched us with

I waved at her and gave her my best smile,

just to see what would happen. She gave me

her best blank expression.

SHE MUST BE THE MEANEST
PERSON ON THE PLANET
AFTER DANIEL GREEN.

When we were on the motorway, Esa started saying he needed to pee.

'But it's only been forty minutes!' said Dad.

Mum said, 'I knew I shouldn't have given you that apple juice.'

Dad said he had to hold it until we got to the services. But Mum said he was only little and couldn't hold it that long. Maryam said, 'We should have put a nappy on him because he's a big fat baby.'

Dad said to stop being so rude.

I hate it when we are stuck in the car and everyone is being all stressed out and I also hate the thought of Esa peeing on the seat right next to me. I mean, how YUCK!

I would end up sitting in a

puddle of his pee.

So I stared out of the window and imagined myself on my roller blades, riding alongside all the cars and faster than them. So fast, that there was

A JET OF FIRE

blazing out the

back of them.

And then I said,

ROLLERBLADES lift off!

And they took me all the way to the moon.
I don't actually have any roller blades, and
I don't know how to roller skate, but that's
the great thing about imagining: you can
do anything you want. Except pee. For that,
we had to stop on the hard shoulder so Esa
could let it out.

I asked my parents why it was called the
hard shoulder. Nobody knew. This is why
my parents should let me have my own
smartphone, because then I could have just
looked it up myself.

That night, while we pretended to be asleep on our row of mattresses on Aunty Sumayyah's living room floor, Reza told me that Daniel was right, all Asians were going to be kicked out of the country and we were probably going to have a WORLD WAR III

I gulped. He told me that we would all have to go and live in Pakistan.

'Have you ever been to Pakistan?' I said.

'Yeah. Once, when I was five.'

'What's it like? Will we like living there?'

I felt sick. **I didn't want to live in a strange place I had never been to.**

The five bars of chocolate that we had snuck into our beds and eaten attempted to make their way back up my throat.

'Well, the pizza is YUCK

and you can hardly understand what people are saying,' Reza said.

'Why?'

'Because they speak in Urdu. You can't speak Urdu, can you?'

'No.'

I lay awake for ages after Reza had fallen asleep. I imagined his quiet snoring sounds were from H_2O instead and that my pillow was resting on H_2O's back. It made me feel better to know that wherever we had to move to, I could take him with me.

At breakfast, there was such a big feast of food on the table that I forgot all about Daniel and Pakistan. Uncle Fahad had even pulled out last night's leftover chicken wings.

What's that? asked Esa.

Meat, said Dad.

Where did it come from?

A chicken.

Did it lay it?

Everyone burst into laughter. Uncle Fahad choked on his juice.

CHAPTER 12

One evening the following week, when we were putting our lasagne-covered dishes into the dishwasher, we heard an

coming down our street. Maryam and I both raced to the window, while Esa whined to be let down from the table (he was still eating, as usual, because he's super slow).

The ambulance lights were flashing so brightly the whole room was lit up.

Maryam and I pressed our faces to the glass. The ambulance had stopped next door and the paramedics were hurrying towards the front door.

'**It's Mrs Rogers!**' I said in surprise.

'Oh no ...' gasped Mum.

Dad had his quick-thinking face on.

'I should go,' said Mum. 'Should I go? I should go.'

Maryam said, 'No way, she's horrible!'

Esa dropped his plate of freezing cold lasagne on the floor with a

Dad looked at it and breathed a sigh and ran his hand through his hair. He does that when he has his thinking face on.

'What if she doesn't want me? What if she sends me away and shouts at me in front of them?' Mum said as she ran around the room putting her scarf on her head and putting her coat on inside out.

'It doesn't matter, darling. You go. At least you will have done the right thing. Go and see if she needs anything at all.'

'She doesn't deserve it,'

said Maryam and she folded her arms and threw herself onto the sofa.

I went to the front door and watched as

Mum hurried out of our gate. She reached the ambulance just as they were wheeling Mrs Rogers out on a trolley. She was clutching her wrist and telling the paramedics how she had slipped in the bathroom.

'I'm here with you,' Mum said softly. 'I mean, if you want.' And then Mum put her hand out so Mrs Rogers could hold it if she wanted.

Mrs Rogers looked really pale and scared. She said in a small voice, 'John isn't here.'

And then she took Mum's hand and tried to *smile*

Later, Mum said that when Mrs Rogers did that, it was easy to forget all about the rotten things that she had said.

When Mum and Mrs Rogers came home in a taxi a few hours later, Dad went over too, to help Mrs Rogers get settled. When they came back he was grinning from ear to ear because he had heard Mrs Rogers on the phone as they were leaving, saying,

CHAPTER 13

All we seemed to talk about in our house for the next little while was how Mrs Rogers was doing.

Does Mrs Rogers need anything from the supermarket?

Should Omar pop over and check Mrs Rogers' TV was working properly?

Should Esa pick some flowers from the garden to cheer Mrs Rogers up?

Now that Mrs Rogers knew we were nice,
she was a TOTALLY
DIFFERENT
PERSON.

She wasn't
CREEPY
and MEAN

any more. She was

❀ Super Happy ❀

whenever we went round to her house. That

made me wonder why she didn't like us in

the first place. Could it be because the fall

made her brain work differently? When I

suggested this to Dad, he laughed and said

that although that was possible, he thought it had more to do with what she had been reading before in the tabloid newspapers about Muslims, whereas now she knew what we were really like. He said we should invite her to our house during Ramadan so she could learn more about the real Islam.

Adults get super excited about Ramadan

which is kind of confusing because during Ramadan you can't eat or drink ALL DAY. I know my mum and dad like to eat a whole lot, and my mum is completely addicted to

coffee. Even though they make up for all the
not eating when they break their fast, at iftar
time, no one had ever really explained to me
what was so good about Ramadan. So I asked
Aunty Iman.

Aunty Iman was my new Qur'an teacher.
She isn't related to us, but Maryam and I
call all ladies that are our mum's age 'Aunty'
because it's rude to just say their name. She
comes over to teach me how to read the
Qur'an every Wednesday and Friday after
school. I like her, because she's kind. She's

WAAAAAY BETTER

than my last teacher from before we moved, who didn't tell me about what the words meant and just told me to be quiet whenever I asked a question about Allah, which made it boring. I like to know what the words mean. I heard my mum telling my dad that the teacher wasn't doing a good job of handling my

INQUISITIVE NATURE.

Anyway, it was super handy that Aunty Iman filled me in on what's so good about Ramadan, because Charlie has an inquisitive nature too, and he started asking me lots of questions all about it.

'So, wait, Omar, in Ramadan, you can't eat for a whole month? Won't people die if they do that?' he asked.

'Hahahaha. No. You only have to stop eating

from dawn till sunset

Basically, when the sun is out. All the
other times, you can eat what you want, and
you can eat lots, like my mum and dad do,
so you stay alive.'

'OK.' Charlie looked a bit relieved but
a bit sheepish too, so I felt a little bad for
laughing. 'But why do people do it? The
fasting, I mean. And if they like doing it, why
do they only do it in Ramadan?'

'Because that's when you're supposed
to do it, and for a whole month you get

extra reward points from Allah. I found out that you get seventy times more points for praying and reading Qur'an than you do in other months.' We were sitting by the sandpit in the playground, so I made two piles with the sand, one that was like a

MASSIVE MOUNTAIN

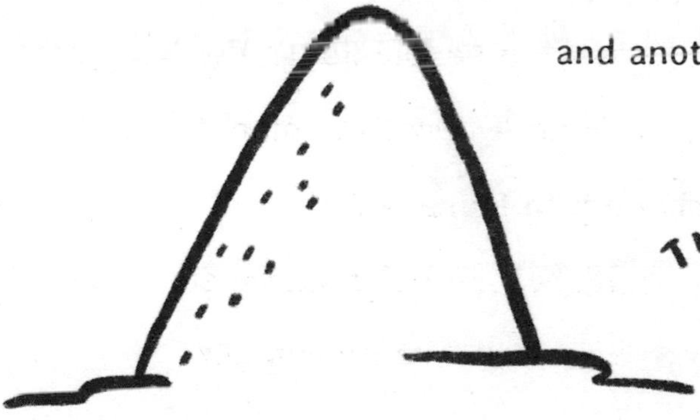

and another

TINY LITTLE ONE.

'OK. That's really cool,' said Charlie. 'Is it hard?'

'I think so. Anyway, even if it's hard, we have the *Eid feast* to look forward to at the end of the month! It also helps that the Devil is locked up during Ramadan, so he can't persuade us to eat when our tummies are rumbling.'

I IMAGINED A 'NASTY' CREATURE GRUMPILY COUNTING DOWN THE DAYS TO RAMADAN BECAUSE HE KNEW HE WAS GOING TO GET LOCKED AWAY

And since it's the Devil who whispers to us to do bad things, I was pretty relieved that I could have a whole month without him telling me to eat Maryam's stash of hidden chocolate when she wasn't looking.

I was planning to ask Allah for a lifetime's supply of chocolate of my own on the

which is in the last ten days of Ramadan. It's called that because it's better than

1000

months. That means you could get the same reward points in one night that it would

take you one thousand months to get! That's
eighty-three years!

MINDBLOWING!

WOW!

And all the angels come down to Earth and
you can ask Allah for anything you want.

Then I remembered the best bit. 'AND for
people who fast, Allah will give them a secret
reward and we don't know what it is!'

'Wow,' said Charlie. 'Maybe like a **FERRARI ITALIA** or something?'

'OH MY GOD, Charlie! That would be so awesome.' I could almost feel the steering wheel in my hands ...

CHAPTER 14

The first fast was on a Monday. Maryam was going to wake up for the **MIDNIGHT FEAST!** because she was going to be fasting for the whole of Ramadan for the first time. The meal is called suhur, and it has to happen before dawn. My mum said that I wasn't allowed to get up for it because I was still too young. I wasn't happy about this at all – I wanted my Ferrari Italia! So I put up a fuss and turned on the turbo on my

PESTER POWER.

In the end, Mum said I could practise keeping a fast at the weekend. I said fine, but I was still worried about Maryam getting more reward points than me.

So I went to school with breakfast in my tummy as usual. It was funny that at school it was just a normal day, when at home it was special because it was the first day of Ramadan and that's all that anyone could talk about. Nobody in my class was talking about it, which is why I was super surprised when Mrs Hutchinson bounced over to my table and said,

'Happy Ramadan, Omar.'

I think my cheeks might have gone red.
But I looked at her, at her Happy Ramadan
curls, and managed a very small thank you.

'Are you fasting?' she continued, crouching
down near my chair.

'No, I'm not allowed,' I said.

'Oh, well,' she said, 'I'm happy to go easy
on you for PE if you ever do.' And she winked
and went to write the date on the board.

The first person I saw when I looked up
was Daniel.

Something was making him red, and fidgety, and really cross.

Could it have been jealousy?

At break time, Daniel came over to where Charlie and I were sitting, doing cool graffiti drawings with chalks on the floor. 'YOU'RE A TEACHER'S PET!' He spat out the words as if they were a really nasty part of a pet, like its poop. And he pointed a podgy finger at me, back and forth, back and forth before smudging up our drawings with his foot.

Anger bubbled up in my chest.

I imagined H_2O swooping down from the clouds and whacking Daniel with his strong tail.

If only he could do that for real ... I was so tired of Daniel using any old excuse to pick on me.

'GO AWAY, DANiEL,' I said.

'What will you do? Call your *girlfriend*, Mrs Hutchinson?'

'She's not his girlfriend, OK?' said Charlie.

For a second, I thought Daniel was going to try his headbutting thing again but, luckily, he saw one of the teaching assistants coming towards us, so he ran away. The teaching assistant walked past us slowly, asking if everything was all right. I said yes, even though it wasn't.

Afterwards, Charlie asked me if we should just go and tell her or Mrs Hutchinson that Daniel was being a big fat bully. I just shook my head. I knew getting Daniel in trouble would only make things worse. But I also knew that I had to do *something* – standing up to Daniel made me feel shaky and sick, and I super definitely didn't want to have to feel that way for ever.

I imagined H_2O flying off into the distance and entering a big fluffy white cloud in the blue sky. I decided that's where he lives. Everyone's seen it, it's the big cloud that is shaped like a dragon. It probably feels like being wrapped up in

balls of cotton wool

like the ones my mum uses on her face. If the cloud wasn't there and the sky was clear blue, it would be because H_2O had gone to visit his friends or buy some

or whatever dragons do in their spare time when their owners don't need them. And when the cloud was darker and spilled rain onto the earth, that would be when H_2O was having a shower.

YOU DIDN'T THINK DRAGONS NEEDED TO WASH?

Well, maybe your dragon doesn't see as much action as my H_2O ...

CHAPTER 15

That evening, Mrs Rogers came over for the first iftar, which is the food you eat when you break your fast at sunset. Her wrist still wasn't all fixed up yet, and Mum and Dad had been sending dinner over to her so that she didn't have to cook for herself. But this was the first time she actually came to eat at our house, on our table.

She watched everything we did, quietly,  with a smile in her eyes. She kept saying,

and nodding her head.

Once we'd finished eating, she took her phone out and called John – who was her son, it turned out – and said, 'The Muslims put less chilli in their food for me, John. It was *delicious.*' We all grinned, because being called the Muslims was a bit of a fun joke for us all now.

As the week went on, I noticed that everyone was getting used to not eating when the sun was out. And, actually, eating a bit too much when the sun went down. Normally, Maryam and I eat about the same amount, but now

SHE WAS EATING LIKE A BEAR WHO HADN'T HAD ANY FOOD FOR THE WHOLE TIME IT HAD BEEN HIBERNATING.

At first, I was worried that she would eat all the *yummy samosas* if I wasn't quick enough, but then I figured out that while she was busy munching, I could talk loads about my video games and she wouldn't tell me to shut up like she normally does.

Mrs Rogers came over for the iftar every day. She told me she liked the samosas best of all.

But by the time we got to Thursday, everyone was a little bit less patient. Probably because they were hungry. It didn't help that Maryam had done really badly in her science test, which was a

COMPLETE CATASTROPHE ☒

in our household because she is the daughter of two successful scientists. Mum was telling her that it really wasn't good enough and that they would go over all the things that she found hard. And Dad was saying that they wouldn't be upset if they didn't believe that Maryam could do better.

I looked at Maryam. Once, I watched a video of a gorilla dad whose gorilla children were being really, really annoying, and he

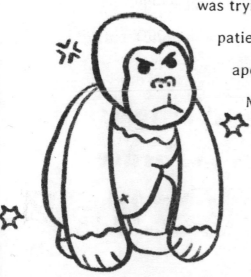 was trying his best to be patient and not to 'go ape', until he DID. Maryam reminded me of the gorilla, trying to stay calm. It didn't last long.

'WELL, IT'S NOT MY FAULT, IS IT? YOU'RE THE ONE WHO MADE ME MOVE TO THIS STUPID SCHOOL AND STUPID HOUSE!'

SHOUTED GORILLA-MARYAM.

'Mummy, I can do better, can't I?' said Esa.

'Of course you can, sweetie,' said Mum.

For this, Maryam pinched Esa as she stormed out of the room. Mum was a bit flustered and didn't seem to notice, but I kept quiet about it because

i might be able to use it against her in future.

Mum said I was sitting around doing nothing, so I should go and set the table for

iftar and take the stones out of the dates
and put nuts in instead. I wondered why
they were called stones and I imagined what
would happen if there were real stones in
dates and somebody tried to eat one, thinking
it had a nut in it. If they didn't smash their
teeth doing that and managed to swallow it
instead, would it stay in their tummies for
ever, or would they poop it out?

Just as I had finished setting the table,
Dad came into the room. He liked that I
had gone over the top and taken out fancy
glasses and made the table look like they
do in restaurants. Mum put her head around
the door. She didn't like it. She said that her
fancy glasses could get broken and that I
shouldn't touch them. Then she told me to go
and get Mrs Rogers to join us for iftar.

Mrs Rogers brought a box of chocolates with her.

It was only twelve steps from her front door to our's, which takes me about twelve seconds to walk across. It takes Mrs. Rogers sixty seconds. I timed it.

That doesn't sound like a lot, but it's really slow when you're doing it with her. While we

walked, I had my eye on the chocolates. How could I make sure that Maryam didn't pinch all the best ones?

Mrs Rogers knew the iftar routine now. When there were only ten minutes left till the fast opened, she said, 'Put the Islam Channel on, or we'll miss that nice song that tells us when the fast opens.'

We all tried not to look at each other and tried not to laugh.

'That's called the adhan, Mrs Rogers,' said Dad. 'It's the call to prayer.'

'Oh well, whatever it's called, it's very nice, dear,' said Mrs Rogers.

Mrs Rogers did the countdown, and everyone popped a date into their mouths when the fast opened. EXCEPT ME!

I popped a chocolate from the box that Mrs Rogers had brought into my mouth. Because my mouth had been waiting for them. And because my mouth likes chocolates very much. But instead of being very happy, my mouth was confused. There was a

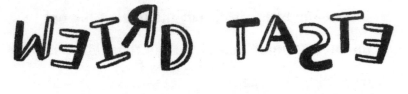

with the chocolate taste.

'YUCK!' I said.

'Oh! Is it an alcohol one?' said Maryam.

We're not allowed alcohol, not even the adults, and I had never had it before. I quickly jumped up to spit it out and rinsed my mouth.

'Am I going to be drunk now?' I asked.

Apparently, this was totally hilarious, because you have to have a lot more alcohol than that to get drunk. Mrs Rogers explained that to me after she finished laughing for ten minutes straight.

CHAPTER 16

When Friday evening finally came round, I was very excited. I had somehow made it to the weekend without getting my bones broken by Daniel AND I was going to be fasting the next day, which meant

I was one step closer to my
FERRARI.

I knew I had to wake up at 2 o'clock in the morning to eat before sunrise. That's

basically the **_middle of the night_**

At first, I couldn't even sleep because I was too excited about getting up when I normally wouldn't be allowed to.

But the next thing I knew, Maryam was waking me up by saying,

'GET UP,

BRAT FACE,'

and poking me in the ribs with long fingers and, for some weird reason, blowing on my face complete with added bits of spit!

Was **SHAYTAN** still whispering to her somehow and making her be mean?

It took me a moment to remember why

I wasn't supposed to be asleep, but then I jumped out of bed.

MiDNiGHT FEAST!

I whizzed down the stairs and jumped onto my seat on the table in the kitchen. Then I jumped right back up to get my favourite cereal.

'How are you this perky, this early in the morning?' said something that sounded a bit like Dad.

Mum and Dad looked different. Like half-zombies. They weren't speaking very much, and when they did, it was just one or two words, and it was a bit slurred.

'Mm, eggs?'

(Usually said as 'Would you like some eggs?')

'H-hot...'

(Usually said as 'Be careful it's hot!')

They were also moving a lot slower than normal. I imagined it was because the whole room was filled with **thick**

zombie

SLIME

and they were wading through it in slow motion.

Adults are funny – I can't understand why they have different levels of energy depending on how much sleep or coffee they've had. I'm basically the same all the time. I think Maryam is on her way to being an adult, because she was at least a quarter-zombie while we were eating suhur.

I had some cereal and was forced to have some egg and porridge too (with biscuit spread, obviously). Then we all went back to bed.

When I woke up on Saturday morning, I had to remember not to eat breakfast and **not to dRink oR eat anything**

I was doing fine till about noon, when my tummy started to rumble a bit. I ignored it and tried to distract myself by building a Lego Triceratops. It worked, because the **{tummy RUMBLiNG}** went away and by the time Dad announced that

we had to get into the Peanut to go to the
supermarket, I had forgotten all about hunger.

That was until we actually reached the
supermarket, and I saw all the shelves
stacked with

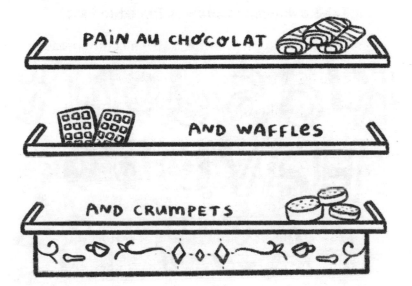

PAIN AU CHOCOLAT

AND WAFFLES

AND CRUMPETS

Even the things I don't normally eat, like
quiche, sat on shelves looking more yummy
than they ever did before. My tummy growled

like H_2O. My insides suddenly ached, and my legs pretended to be jelly sticks.

On the drive back, I asked Dad if I could break my fast. He said that I could, because I was just a kid, and at least I had tried. He said there was a reason why Allah said that

KiDS doN't HaVE To FaSt 👍

Their bodies aren't like adult bodies.

'But are you sure that Allah won't mind?' I asked.

He said of course Allah wouldn't mind and that Allah would just be happy that I had wanted to try in the first place.

'You can always try again next weekend, if you like.'

That made me happy. I took a pain au chocolat out of the bag next to me and took a big bite.

Just for the record. I did try again next weekend, and I kept a whole fast. I've been looking forward to my ∹FERRARI ITALIA∹ ever since.

CHAPTER 17

We'd been living in our new house for seven whole weeks. That doesn't sound like a lot, but it was weird:

MY BEDROOM REALLY FELT LIKE MY BEDROOM NOW.

Even though when I shut my eyes I could still remember exactly how my old room looked, with the stickers on the wardrobe that were peeling off, and the glow-in-the-dark stars on the ceiling that Dad helped me put up when I was younger, and Esa's teddies all over the floor. I didn't feel like I wanted to move back. I liked pretty much everything about where we lived now.

Everything except ... Can you guess?

Daniel obviously.

Nobody else seemed to have a problem with me, but Daniel kept ruining everything. Most of our class hung out together in the playground, and though Charlie was my best friend we often played football with Filip and Jayden and Jessica. Once or twice, the girls on the table next to ours even asked for my help in science, *even* Sarah, who is smart at everything.

I'll give you an example of how Daniel
made me feel miserable about

A MILLION

pointless things. One Wednesday afternoon,
Mrs Hutchinson asked a question. It was the
type of question that teachers ask when they
know that the kids won't know the answer,
but they ask it anyway, just to see.

She asked, 'What is DNA?'

The class was blank. I knew Mrs
Hutchinson had expected that because she
didn't look disappointed. I knew what it was,
but I didn't want to be a show-off.

'OK, does anybody know what genes are?'
she said.

One kid put his hand up and proudly said, 'Clothes.'

'No ...' she said slowly, stretching it out, which meant she wanted other guesses.

'Genies?' asked another kid, clearly unsure.

Mrs Hutchinson's face still smiled, but her hair and eyes gave it away. She was sad her class didn't have at least a clue about what genes were.

I COULDN'T TAKE IT ANY MORE. I SHOT MY HAND UP.

'Genes are what make us what we are. They're like special instructions. They decide what colour our eyes are, and things like that. And DNA is where the genes are found. Lots of them!'

Mrs Hutchinson's hair sprang to life, like flowers which had just been watered.

She said she was astonished at how much I knew about genes. I told her my parents were both scientists and it was kind of their favourite topic.

Charlie gave me a high-five.

But then Daniel gave me a **ROTTEN** look, and suddenly I wished I'd never said anything at all. Every time he glared at me, or pushed me and Charlie around in the playground it reminded me of what he'd said – that

I SHOULD BE KICKED OUT OF MY HOME,

and sent to a country I'd never even visited. I didn't *think* he could be right, but if he wasn't then why would Reza believe it was going to happen too?

At home things were just as normal. Everyone was settled into the Ramadan routine and starting to plan for Eid, which was just around the corner. We have two Eids in the year and they are the two best days of the year for me. There's *Eid ul-Fitr* which was the Eid coming up, the one that is for celebrating that we've fasted for a whole month and earned lots of reward points. And then there is *Eid al-Adha* just a couple of months later, which basically celebrates Hajj – that's when people go to

Makkah

on a holy journey. We have to sacrifice a sheep or something on that Eid, like Prophet Abraham did, but obviously if you don't have a farm you can't do it yourself.

If I had to choose, my favourite Eid is the first one, because that's when I seem to get

A WHOLE LOT MORE PRESENTS

Maybe by the second one everyone's money has run out or something.

I usually drop a lot of hints to my parents about what presents to get me.

Pleeeeeeease can I have an Xbox One? Pleeease?

OK, maybe it's not hinting. Maybe it's begging.

My mum orders lots of the presents and Eid clothes online. But it's funny, because when the delivery man comes, she runs around the house going AARRGGGHHH and looking for her headscarf. Which is never 'where she left it'. It usually involves her hopping from room to room before sprinting upstairs to grab one and opening the door panting and apologising. Once or twice, she's even grabbed my hoody and used it as a hijab.

The last time this happened, Maryam pointed out that people who aren't Muslim must think that Muslim women wear their scarves on their heads

ALL DAY LONG

Even at home. Because whenever she comes to the door, Mum always has one on. They must think **Mum sleeps in it** and **showers in it** and *eats her* **breakfast** in it. When Maryam isn't being

Princess Grumpy-Pants

she can be really funny. The thought of Mum

showering in her headscarf had us laughing
for literally seven and a half minutes. I kept
imagining her shampooing it and blow-
drying it. And then at dinner, out of the blue,
Maryam blurted out

'SH◉WER SCARF!'

and I spat my food all over the table because
I laughed so hard.

CHAPTER 18

Have you ever gone on a school trip but never quite made it to where you were supposed to be going? If you haven't, you're lucky. Me?

I SEEM TO BE A MAGNET FOR TROUBLE.

My class was supposed to be going to the Science Museum. My parents were obviously extremely excited about this. The Science Museum had a new section called the Wonderlab which Mum and Dad took us to see as soon as it opened. But it was super cool, so I didn't mind going again. Especially because they have these slides made out of different materials, to teach you about friction, and one of them is really fast.

SO FAST THAT i ALMOST PEED MYSELF LAUGHiNG

the first time I went on it.

We were put into groups of six for the trip. A teaching assistant or a parent was in charge of each group. I could tell Mrs Hutchinson was stressed that morning because some curls from her hair were looking pretty and in place, and others were sticking out in funny directions – completely ignoring gravity.

I listened as she read out names for the groups.

" MY HEART WAS THUDDING IN MY CHEST. "

I had my fingers crossed under the table, because I really didn't want to be in Daniel's group. I knew I wasn't supposed to believe in crossing fingers. But I was trying anything. It was only later that I realised I didn't even ask Allah not to put me in Daniel's group. My mum said that if I had, Allah might have put me in a different group, or he might have even still put me in Daniel's group because

He works in mysterious ways.

As you've probably guessed, I was put in a group with Daniel. And Charlie was put in a whole different group.

OUCH!

When our names were announced, Daniel looked over at me and snarled. The worst bit was that it wasn't even a teacher in charge of our group. It was just another kid's parent. And she had no idea which kids were

TROUBLEMAKERS

and which were not.

Charlie came up to me and said, 'Don't

worry, OK? We can still look at things together in the museum, OK?'

I said, 'OK,' too. I was feeling too miserable to say anything else.

To get to the museum, we had to go on the London Underground. It was going pretty all right, until we tried to change trains.

DANIEL WAS LIKE A LION WAITING TO POUNCE.

As soon as we switched platforms, in the rush of people, he took hold of the belt of my trousers and jerked me back.

'Your girlfriend Charlie can't save you now,' he barked.

Have you ever wanted to laugh in a horrible situation? I don't know why, but

I CRACKED UP -LAUGHING

even though I was probably about to get hit by the worst bully I'd ever met. It was a weird kind of not-real-laugh, though, and it just seemed to make Daniel more furious.

'Oh, so you think it's funny, do you, teacher's pet?!'

People in dark suits and smart shoes were walking past us as if nothing out of the ordinary was going on.

'Our group! The class! We'll get left behind!' I finally managed to squeak.

Daniel looked over, and saw what I saw: a crowd of busy-looking people exiting the platform, but nobody from our school. He seemed to freeze. Then, just a few seconds later, we were the only two people left.

What happened next was completely astonishing.

Daniel started wailing like a baby.

'WAAAAAA! WE'RE LOST. WE'RE GOING TO DIE.'

I realised that I was going to have to handle this situation. And take care of the big crying bully baby in front of me even though Daniel was making me want to cry, too. I had been on the London Underground with my

parents millions of times. But never on my

own. It looked different now that I was on my

own. It looked bigger. Noisier. Darker. *Scarier.*

And it smelled of wee.

No, wait, that was Daniel.

He had weed himself.

CHAPTER 19

I know we should have tried to find
somebody who worked at the station to help,
but my thinking wasn't very straight at that
time. It was kind of WOBBLY
and I was getting like a gazillion different
ideas of what to do every second. That's a

very noisy
head and,
don't forget,
Daniel was
still crying.

A train  **RUMBLED ONTO THE PLATFORM**

from the tunnel, and my instinct was to jump on.

Instincts are funny. You hear about them with animals, like when sea turtles hatch and move towards the ocean without anybody telling them which way to go. Or when baby kangaroos jump into their mummy kangaroo's pouch when they are born. I felt myself wanting to **JUMP** onto that train, although nobody had told me it was the right way to go.

I took Daniel's hand, trying very hard not to think about when he had **picked his nose** earlier, and stepped on.

It was South Kensington station we were supposed to be going to. I remembered Mrs Hutchinson saying so and I remembered that when I went to the museum with Mum and Dad we had to walk quite a lot through the station to get out near where the museums were.

Daniel and I found seats on the train.

'Do you know where to go?' sobbed Daniel.

'Yes, look on that map up there,' I said, pointing towards the one that shows all the stops. 'See if you can find South Kensington on it.'

We looked. Very carefully. Marylebone
station came. We still searched the map,
but South Kensington was nowhere on that
brown line. My heart sank as I said to Daniel:

I love the Peanut, but suddenly I wished
that we went to more places on the train, so I
would know what I was doing.

'Let's tell someone we're lost,' pleaded
Daniel.

'No. We're not lost,' I said. I kind of knew
we were, but I wanted to get us out of the
mess. Now that Daniel was all snivelly and

depending on me, I wanted to be a

'We just have to get off this train,' I said.
'Then we'll be fine.'

We got off at the next stop. It was Baker
Street. Baker Street sounded very familiar.
It sounded like home and good memories. I
thought maybe it was another station that
was close to the museums, and that's why I
remembered it.

Daniel was like a  **BIG LUMP OF PLAY DOUGH**

that couldn't think. I had to do all the thinking. But it sort of felt OK – he wasn't being mean to me any more, at least.

I wondered whether our class knew we were missing by now. I imagined Mrs Hutchinson's hair going crazy with worry. I had never seen her really worried before and I wondered what it looked like.

We exited the station, crossed over at a pelican crossing and walked down a busy road with lots of cafes on it. There was a Sherlock Holmes museum. I don't know much about Sherlock, but my parents are crazy about a TV show about him that has Benedict Cumberbatch in it. Another thing I know about Benedict Cumberbatch is that he can't say the word 'penguin'. I only know this because one time when I walked into the kitchen, my mum was watching a video about him and laughing so much that tears were falling from her eyes.

The road started winding to the left and as we turned the corner, something touched my shoulder from behind. I swung my head around, and what I saw made me

like a hyena who was about to be eaten by a

bigger, scarier creature for dinner.

ΣAM

CHAPTER 20

It was the scariest thing I'd ever seen. It was terrifying and hairy and it stank. It stank so bad. It was kind of like a man, because it had a head and a body and arms and legs. But it wasn't a man. And it was dirty. So dirty. My brain told me it was a ...

ZOMBIEEEEEE!

Daniel screamed too.

We both ran down a long road. I looked over my shoulder. The zombie was still coming, with its arm out, trying to grab us. I ran harder.

When I couldn't see him any more, I stopped and tried to catch my breath.

Daniel, on the other hand, **threw himself onto the pavement** and started wailing like never before.

I wasn't well trained in dealing with crying bullies, or zombies. I took a deep breath and imagined H_2O flying down to help us. Swooping around to keep an eye out in case the zombie turned up again.

And then I sat down next to Daniel on the pavement. Even though there was loads of gross dried-up chewing gum on it.

I told him it was going to be OK. When I said that, I felt like a liar, because I was scared too, and I didn't really know if it was going to be OK. But that's what grown-ups always say when someone is crying – so I said it.

GROWN-UPS! What would they do right now?

'Daniel, what would your parents do if they were lost?'

Daniel wiped some snot from his nose, with the back of his hand. 'They would look for the way on their phones.'

'Right. We don't have phones.'

'What would yours do? If they were in trouble and were going to die, like us?'

I had to try very hard not to laugh at how dramatic Daniel was being. He actually thought this was the end of the world. Well, the zombie thing was quite scary. But H_2O didn't have to hold back, so I imagined him rolling on the floor laughing instead.

'Well, any time there's a big problem, my parents always ask Allah. That's one thing they keep telling me a lot, to ask Allah for everything. They say it every day.'

Daniel sat up. There was something suddenly different about his face.

I think it was

- hope -

'And did you?' he asked.

'Ermm. Actually, no. I forgot,' I said sheepishly.

'Ask him!' shouted Daniel. And for a moment, I thought he was going to become the bully Daniel again. But he just sat there waiting, with

BiG, HOPEFUL EYES

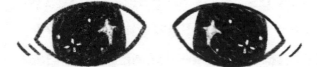

I closed my eyes and whispered a few words, in English. I didn't know the exact Arabic prayer for being lost with a bully and being chased by a zombie, but my dad said that Allah knows all the languages in the universe, so we can talk to him however we need to.

Allah, I'm sorry I forgot to ask you before, but we're kind of lost, and we need your help. We lost all our teachers and we don't know where they are. We don't even know where WE are actually. And also, there might be a zombie trying to catch us. I'm trying to look after Daniel, but he keeps crying a lot. Please, can you help us. I don't know how, but I guess you Know. Thank you. I love you.

I opened my eyes to find Daniel's face

right next to mine. 'Well? Did you ask him? Is

he going to help us?'

'Of course He will, Allah always helps.'

'But do you think he heard you? You were whispering so quietly I couldn't even hear you, and I'm right next to you.'

'Yes, He did. He's God!' I said in my

WELL, DUHHHH ~

voice, but then I realised I should be kinder, and explained, 'God can hear everything, even whispers and even what you're saying to yourself in your own head.'

'Oh, OK,' said Daniel.

Then, because Daniel still looked so frightened and sad, I said, 'Don't worry, you'll get back home to your mum and dad, and so will I.'

'Yeah, if they even notice I'm gone, or if

they even care,' said Daniel.

'Of course they care. That's what parents do. Anyway, I think you're a bit hard to miss. I mean, if you weren't there, *I* would notice.'

'Really?'

'SUPER DEFINITELY.'

Daniel seemed pleased to hear that, for like 0.8 seconds, then his shoulders drooped again.

'Yes but ... my parents ... all they care about is my little sister, Suzy. Because she's always in hospital.'

'Is she ... is she going to be OK?'

'I don't know, she's always sick and having operations ...' He started wailing again, as if something was hurting a whole lot. 'And I do care about her, I do. I do ... But, what about me? I might as well not be there. I just get in the way when they need to look after her.'

Poor Daniel. **I felt a little lump in my throat**. And I stared at him because I didn't know what to say. So I just moved closer to him, even though he stank of pee, and I said, 'I don't know what I would do if that happened to me.'

Daniel looked at me as if I had said something that really, really helped. But I had just said the truth, because I didn't know what else to say. He sniffed really hard and wiped his eyes before looking up at me like he was waiting for me to say more. So, I said, 'Yeah. You must be **A REALLY STRONG PERSON**

I mean like strong inside, not strong like

BATMAN

although I think Batman is strong inside as well.'

Daniel smiled a snotty smile.

Is this the first time he's ever smiled at me?
I thought. That felt really weird. Didn't he
hate me?

'So, what now? Do we just sit here?' asked
Daniel.

'I don't think so. The ZOMBIE
might find us.'

'What then?'

'Let's walk.'

CHAPTER 21

So we got up and carried on walking the same way we'd been going before.

Daniel was calmer now. I was kind of proud of him, and of myself. Even though he did smell because of the pee in his pants.

After we'd walked for a few minutes, I knew. I knew why this place was so familiar.

I took Daniel's hand and started running. And there it was: the huge dome of

London Central Mosque

I loved this mosque. This was where I had had my first halal sweets. This was where a man had given me £10, just for being cute. This was where I had stood many times, sometimes with Mum and sometimes with Dad, and with hundreds of other people, all praying at the same time. This place was safe.

We ran and ran till we reached the big space outside the mosque, where I had tried to ride my scooter once. I looked over my shoulder, and ...

AAARRR...

The zombie was hot on our heels again.
How did he do that?!

We pumped up the screaming even more
and ran right into the mosque. Mosques are
usually quiet places, so all the commotion
made people come out from their places and
come up to us.

There was a man who
was wearing one of those
Arab-style long things that
go right down to the feet.
I had one in white. My
grandma bought it for me
from Makkah. The man had
lots of wrinkles and lots

···GGGHHH

of white hair and he was using his hands to signal us to calm down. He was also saying something, but I couldn't hear him, because we were still screaming.

So I stopped.
Then Daniel stopped.

Then I told him everything. It was weird – I felt like I could hear my own voice from far away and it sounded really hysterical. I told him we had got lost and tried to find our own way to the Science Museum and then we'd got chased by a zombie. Then I realised

iT ALL SOUNDED SUPER CRAZY,

so I quickly told him that we asked Allah for

help and ended up here.

The man smiled, like he was very proud of us and like he knew all the secrets of the world.

'And where is this zombie, my child?' he asked.

Before I could look around to see where he was, Daniel started pointing and squealing, 'There, he's there!'

The man gently took my shoulders and made me look again.

'My dear son,' he said. (I wasn't his son, but sometimes people in the mosque who don't know you love you like you're their son.) 'That is no zombie. That is a homeless man. And it looks as if he was trying to help you.'

I felt like a complete SillyHeAd

because it WAS a homeless man. And he wasn't chasing us. He had just noticed that we were kids, all by ourselves, and he actually cared enough to try to help – but we had run away from him.

I felt pretty bad. I waved at the homeless man sheepishly and he waved back and gave me a yellow-toothed grin. Somebody had sat him down with a cup of tea.

Then the man in the thobe, whose name was Mohamed, sat us down and called our school. A younger man, in jeans and a T-shirt that said  came over and gave us some juice and

halal sweets

This made Daniel's day. (It made mine too.)

I felt pretty good at this point.

I FELT MORE
THE HERO
I WAS TRYING
TO BE.

The school had been frantic and had already called the police. Apparently, everyone had been going nuts with worry, especially poor Charlie, and both Daniel's parents and mine had been told.

A policeman and a policewoman showed up about ten minutes later to talk to us. We also got to talk to Eddy, the homeless not-so-zombie man. He was very smiley, even though he doesn't own many clothes or have a house to live in.

'I would've been able to catch up with you if it wasn't for my bad knee!'

he laughed.

As soon as he spoke, I liked him, because he had an accent from up North that sounded just like Reza's. We told him we were sorry for running away from him, and offered him some of our sweets. He liked the red ones the best, just like every one else I know.

Next, our parents turned up. First mine, and then Daniel's. My mum held onto me and cried and cried, and my dad held onto her.

Everyone decided that it was best that we didn't go to the Wonderlab, as we had had enough adventures for the day. Daniel and I didn't mind. I wondered if he just wanted to stay near his mum, like I did.

Then Dad said, 'Come on, Trouble. Let's get you home.' And he kidnapped me on his shoulder just to make me laugh.

CHAPTER 22

When everything had settled down that evening, Charlie's mum rang my mum and asked if she could bring Charlie over to see me, because

he was a panicky mess

and wanted to make sure I was OK with his own eyes.

So Charlie came over, and we ate biscuits with chocolate milk and I told him all about the zombie thing and about Daniel peeing himself. Then after we finished almost peeing *ourselves* with laughter, I sat up straight

and told Charlie that I felt bad for laughing,

because **Daniel wasn't too bad at all,**

now that I had got to know him a bit.

'OK?' said Charlie.

But he didn't seem too sure, so I said,

'You'll see. Scout's honour!' and saluted at

him. I wasn't a Scout, and Charlie just

**bURST OuT
LAuGHiNG**

again, but I think he believed me.

A couple of days later, my parents invited

Daniel and his family to our house for iftar.

They all wanted to discuss every detail of that

of being lost on the underground. Mr and Mrs

Green seemed nice. **I remembered**

what Daniel had said about

feeling like he was just in

the way at home. But they were

paying him lots of attention now. His dad

kept ruffling his hair, and his mum kept

touching his shoulder like she wanted to

check he was still there. I had a feeling that

that was why they'd left his sister Suzy with

her aunt for this visit, so Daniel could be

their star. They told Mum and Dad that they

were very grateful to the mosque for helping us. Then Daniel told my parents all about how I asked Allah for help and it was only after that that we were saved, so it must have been Allah that did it.

Of course, I had already told them my version of the story, but they were

extra proud

to hear it from him.

Daniel's parents wanted to go to the mosque to thank them again personally, so we had the idea that they should come with us on Eid day and do it then.

Everything was looking really good. I could hardly believe that in just a few days, Daniel

had gone from being the person I liked least
of all to being my friend. He was trying to be
Charlie's friend too, which was a bit harder
because they're

SOOOOOO **DiFFERENT**

to each other. But I

had been an

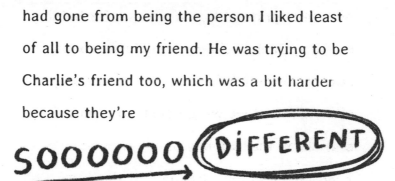

ACCIDENTAL
MAGNET

again and pulled them

together and I was

completely super sure

they'd get on. Charlie

and I even asked Daniel to play football with

us in the playground, because we realised

that nobody had even asked him before. It

turned out that he was better than anyone in

the whole class at being goalie. But there was

still one thing that was bothering me, so I

just blurted it out:

'WILL THE ASIANS
BE KICKED OUT
OF THE COUNTRY?'

The air in the room suddenly got very

thick, like we were on a

DiffERENT
PLANET

with less oxygen or something. Everyone
looked very awkward. And since Maryam
always giggles in awkward situations, she
put her hand over her mouth, but I could still
see her shoulders shaking and so could Esa,
because he pointed at her with his cheeky grin.

'Where did you get an idea like that?'
said Dad.

'ERMMMM,' I suddenly
realised that I'd got it from Daniel, but Daniel
would be in trouble if I said anything. I
looked at him really quickly and looked away,
then I said, 'I, erm, heard it somewhere and I
even asked Reza, and he said we will have to
live in Pakistan.'

Dad laughed, but Mum nudged him
because she could see that I was serious.
Then she smiled politely at the Greens, who

looked really uncomfortable. Daniel was

colour-matching his skin with the

on the plate. I wondered if he could feel it

when he went red.

Dad explained that that was never going to

happen, and kids make things up all the time. He

said that I should always talk to an adult to get

the facts right when I hear something like that.

Then Daniel blurted out, '**OK!**

It was me.
And I'm sorry, Omar.'

Everyone's heads turned to Daniel really

fast. Daniel's head hung towards the floor.

'Well, I heard my cousin Brian saying it, so

I just said it to Omar to make him feel bad

because I didn't think he'd want to be my

friend. But I'm sorry now, anyway.'

Mrs Green's face was doing the colour-

matching thing with the tomatoes now.

And Mr Green was saying, 'Oh,

Daniel.' And he was burying his face in his

hands.

And then Mrs Green was saying, 'I'm so,

so sorry.'

And Daniel was saying, 'I'm so, so sorry.'

And Dad was saying, 'Hey, it's OK. Kids will be kids.'

And Mum was looking from one person's face to another's.

And then, suddenly, they all went quiet and looked at me.

'Omar, I am very proud that you are Daniel's friend and I wouldn't want you going anywhere,' Mr Green said.

Phew, I thought.

NOW everything IS OK.

I imagined H_2O peeking in through the window. He was tiny now, because I didn't need a huge dragon to make me feel better any more. He winked at me and waved with his tail, before flying back off into his cloud.

CHAPTER 23

It was one of the best days of the year – Eid!

And we were going to spend this one with

Mrs Rogers and the Greens. The night before,

I had stood at my window

TRYING TO SPOT *the moon?*

really, really hoping it would be Eid. The

moon tells us when Ramadan is over,

because it's a new month in the Islamic

calendar. If the new moon can't be seen,

it's basically not Eid for another day. When that happens, it's

SO ANNOYING!

The mosque is always very busy on Eid day. Even people who don't normally go to the mosque to pray, go on Eid day. So it is absolutely PACKED.

We sat on the carpet, waiting for the prayers to start and watching the people pour in. I like how every single person is different. Different shapes and different sizes, even for adults. Like, fully grown adults can be really TALL or quite SHORT And you can get really tall thin ones (who remind me of the BFG) and short large ones and all the sizes in between.

Then (ALL) the different types of faces and shades of colours.

The mosque is great, because you get all types of people all in one place and you're usually sitting still for a while, so it's the perfect place to people-watch.

One thing I've figured out is that some people have the kind of faces that seem quite perfect – they have a straight nose, and maybe good skin and nice lips – but they still don't look *nice*. Like, I wouldn't want to be stuck in a lift with them. And they definitely don't smile a lot. Then there are other faces that might have skin that's a bit bad, and maybe their nose isn't the prettiest, or their beard grows in funny directions

– but they look really nice! And they SMILE loads. I've thought about it a lot, and I think it's all to do with what's happening *inside people*. If they're always having nice thoughts and are good and kind people, they always look lovely, no matter what. And if they're horrid people with rotten thoughts, they'll look horrible. Daniel had been smiling a lot more since we got lost together, and his face was definitely looking much **nicer.**

While the imam led the prayers, the Greens
watched from the back. Afterwards, they
said it was absolutely beautiful, like nothing
they've ever seen before.

Next, we were all going to our home for an

Eid Feast
and Presents!

That's the best part of Eid. We had presents
for Daniel and his family too, even Suzy, who
had joined us this time.

Daniel rode with me in the Peanut, and on
the way he pulled out a little wrapped gift
from his jacket pocket and grinned at me.

'It's another Eid present, but for Charlie. It's
a Batman keyring ... Do you think he'll like it?'

'Super definitely.' I grinned back.

The feast covered every single centimetre

of our dining table, which we call the Eid Table on Eid. We always put piles and piles of things on the Eid Table because we have lots of friends and family to visit. This year there was:

BIRYANI

SAMOSAS

PAKORAS

ROASTED LEG OF LAMB

and CHICKPEAS IN YOGURT

But what my mouth wanted most of all were the sweet desserts like the delicious Pakistani

thing my mum makes with vermicelli
and milk, called SAVAYYAN
and Maryam's special

CHOCOLATE
BROWNIES

Maryam might be super annoying most of
the time, but she's getting REALLY good at
baking brownies ...

I sneaked one for myself and one for
Daniel before Esa licked them all, like he
always does.

'Quick, eat it before anyone else comes in!'

I LAUGHED
OUT LOUD

Daniel gobbled his so fast he got bits of brownie all over his teeth.

'HMNFWHAT?' mumbled Daniel, still with his mouth full.

'Your ... teeth ... are ... so ... brown!' I snorted.

Daniel started laughing too.

'So are yours!'

**DON'T MISS
THE NEXT**

ADVENTURE!

ZANIB MIAN grew up in London and still lives there today. She was a science teacher for a few years after leaving university but, right from when she was a little girl, her passion was writing stories and poetry. She has released lots of picture books with the independent publisher Sweet Apple Publishers, but *Planet Omar* is the first time she's written for older readers.

Planet Omar was first released under the title *The Muslims*, and won the Little Rebels Award 2018, as well as being shortlisted for the UKLA Award and nominated for the CILIP Carnegie Medal.

NASAYA MAFARIDIK is based in Indonesia. Self-taught, she has a passion for books and bright, colourful stationery. *Planet Omar: Accidental Trouble Magnet* is the first time she's collaborated with an author, and she's so excited to see what happens next in the series!